Dedicated to my Dad,
who never told me to "pick something else."

copyright © by Maryanna Hoggatt 2017

First Overcup Press printing, April 2017

OvercupPress
4207 SE Woodstock Blvd. # 253
Portland, OR 97206

PRODUCTION DATE: 9.19.16
BATCH NUMBER: 55477-0 / 801065 R2
PLANT LOCATION: Everbest Printing Co. Ltd. Nansha, China.

ISBN: 978-0983491750

Library of Congress Cataloging-in-Publication
Data is on file with Publisher.

maryannahoggatt.com

overcupbooks.com

TOLLY

D.P.S.

TO: TOLLY Peppercorn
3RD MUSHROOM on RIGHT
Tulip Patch, SHROOM FOREST

Maryanna Hoggatt

TOLLY
is a
BATTLE
RACCOON.

He wants to be the BRAVEST of the BRAVE.

Tolly is starting a new job: Dream Protector.

He is excited, but nervous.

Tolly's first task
is to take a newborn Dream
all the way to Heart Mountain.

Only there can the Dream come true.

But Tolly doesn't know what time
the Dream will be born. So he waits...

and watches...and waits...

hoping, hoping...

...until finally,
he sees a sign!

The Dream is born.

Tolly has until
sunset
to deliver the Dream
to Heart Mountain.

Tolly greets the new Dream warmly and helps it climb into his Basket.

Gathering his courage, Tolly sets off. First, they march through Thought Tunnel...

...then SCRAMBLE down the ROCKS of Sleepy Cliffs...

...and PADDLE across the SWIRLING WATERS of Ruby River.

The journey is long and tiresome.
TOLLY has NEVER gone this FAR before.

He sings to the Dream to keep their spirits up.

They enter the forest of Enemy Wilds.
It's very dark and scary.

Tolly wants to turn around,
but it's the only way to Heart Mountain.

TOLLY stops singing.

They go deeper into the woods.
Suddenly, FEAR and DOUBT CREEP out of the shadows, Reaching for the DREAM.

TOLLY is very frightened.

He thought he could be brave,
but all he wants to do is go home.
He covers his head
and shuts his eyes tight.

Just then, TOLLY hears a tiny voice in the darkness.
The Dream speaks for the first time.

you can do it, TOLLY!

Tolly believes the Dream.

His courage returns and he leaps into the air.

Tolly raises his wooden sword and cries out to the shadows.

"YOU ARE BANISHED!"

Triumphant, Tolly marches out of the forest. They have no time to lose.

They reach the trail to Heart Mountain at last. Tolly helps the Dream climb out of the basket.

Tolly and the Dream hike up the path together.
Are they REALLY nearly there?

They REACH the mountaintop as the sun is setting.
It's time to say goodbye.

"Thank you, TOLLY," says the DREAM. "Now I can come TRUE!
You TRULY are the bRAVEST of the bRAVE."

As the Dream SAILS away, TOLLY feels PROUD.

He watches the STARS light up the night sky,
then turns to go home. His first day
as a DREAM Protector was a success.